Bobby Baboon's Banana Be-Bop

by Barbara deRubertis • illustrated by R.W. Alley

THE KANE PRESS / NEW YORK

Alpha Betty's Class

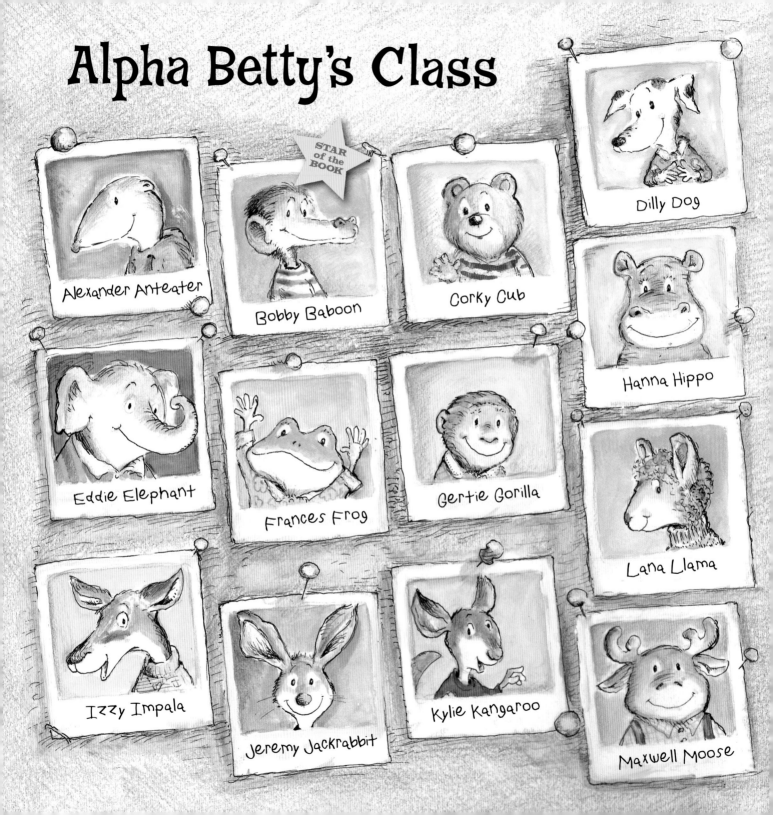

STAR of the BOOK

Alexander Anteater

Bobby Baboon

Corky Cub

Dilly Dog

Eddie Elephant

Frances Frog

Gertie Gorilla

Hanna Hippo

Lana Llama

Izzy Impala

Jeremy Jackrabbit

Kylie Kangaroo

Maxwell Moose

Nina Nandu

Oliver Otter

Polly Porcupine

Quentin Quokka

Rosie Raccoon

Sammy Skunk

Tessa Tiger

Umma Ungka

Victor Vicuna

Walter Warthog

Xavier Ox

Yoko Yak

Zachary Zebra

Alpha Betty

Library of Congress Cataloging-in-Publication Data

deRubertis, Barbara.
Bobby Baboon's banana be-bop / by Barbara deRubertis ; illustrated by R.W. Alley.
p. cm. — (Animal antics A to Z)
Summary: Bobby Baboon brings bananas to give to his classmates at Alpha Betty's school, and, with the help
of some friends, he figures out that he can share the extras.
ISBN 978-1-57565-305-1 (library binding : alk. paper) — ISBN 978-1-57565-301-3 (pbk. : alk. paper)
[1. Baboons—Fiction. 2. Schools—Fiction. 3. Animals—Fiction. 4. Counting—Fiction. 5. Alphabet.
6. Humorous stories.] I. Alley, R. W. (Robert W.), ill. II. Title.
PZ7.D4475Bo 2010
[E]—dc22   2009025207

10 9 8 7 6 5 4 3 2 1

First published in the United States of America in 2010 by Kane Press, Inc.
Printed in Hong Kong
Reinforced Library Binding by Muscle Bound Bindery, Minneapolis, MN

Series Editor: Juliana Hanford
Book Design: Edward Miller

Animal Antics A to Z is a trademark of Kane Press, Inc.

www.kanepress.com

Bobby Baboon picked three big bunches of bananas.

He balanced them in a tub on his head.

Bobby was bringing the bananas to his class at Alpha Betty's school.

As Bobby boogied and be-bopped to school, Bubba Bear called to him.

"Please give me a bunch of those bananas.

I've been sleeping all winter, and I'm HUNGRY.

I'd love a big banana breakfast."

"Boy-oh-boy-oh-boy," said Bobby Baboon.

"I'd be happy to give you all my EXTRA bananas, Bubba!

Let's see. I need one banana for each boy and girl in my class.

If there are 26 boys and girls, how many bananas will I need?"

Bubba Bear rubbed his brow.

"Boy, Bobby, I'm baffled!

That's a big question for my little bear brain.

Let's ask Barnaby Badger for help
with this one. He has a BIG brain!"

"Baaar-naaa-beee!" called Bobby and Bubba.

"Come help us, please!"

Barnaby stumbled and tumbled
down the bank.

Out of breath, he asked,
"May I be of service?"

"Yes, please!" said Bobby Baboon.

"There are 26 boys and girls in my class. I want to give one banana to each of them.

How many bananas do I need?"

Barnaby smiled.

"You need 26 bananas, of course!" he said.

"How many do you have in your tub?"

Bobby Baboon put the three bunches
of bananas on a bench.

Bobby, Bubba, and Barnaby began
counting the bananas in each bunch.

Suddenly a booming voice blasted them from behind.

It said, "Buster Buffalo likes bananas, too!

Give. Me. Bananas. NOW."

Buster Buffalo rumbled and bumbled up to the bench.

He banged his boots on the ground.

He bumped his horns on a bush.

"Don't be a bully, Buster!" said Barnaby Badger bravely.

"Bobby needs 26 bananas for the boys and girls at Alpha Betty's school.

And NOBODY is taking their bananas."

Buster quickly backed off.

Bobby Baboon spoke up.
"We need to count these bananas, Buster.
"Can you help us?"

Buster took a deep breath.
Then he boomed, "You bet, Bobby!"

Bobby's buddies began to count.

"This bunch has 10," beamed Bubba Bear.
"This bunch has 10," beamed Barnaby Badger.
"This bunch has 10," boomed Buster Buffalo.

"Oh, BOY!" said Bobby Baboon.

"That's 10 . . . 20 . . . 30 bananas!

I need only 26 bananas for my class.

So you may have the 4 extra bananas, Bubba!"

"No," said Bubba Bear.

"I'll take only one banana.

I'll give Barnaby one.

I'll give Buster one.

And you can give one
to Alpha Betty!"

"You're a beautiful bear, Bubba,"
Buster Buffalo blubbered.

"I'm sorry I was being a bully."

Bobby Baboon did the banana be-bop all the way to Alpha Betty's school.

Bubba Bear, Barnaby Badger, and Buster Buffalo boogied right along behind him.

The boys and girls at Alpha Betty's school
were always happy to see Bobby arrive.

They liked his be-bop dance.

They liked his bubbling laugh.

And they liked his big bunches of bananas!

"Rub-a-dub-dub!" the boys and girls cried. "Bananas in a tub!

Bravo for Bobby Baboon!"

FUN FACTS

- Home: Africa, usually in grassy lands
- Appearance: Baboons have thick fur on their bodies—but not on their faces.
- Favorite foods: Fruits! But they eat many other foods, too.
- Chatterboxes: Baboons talk to each other with loud screeches, barks, and calls.
- **Did You Know?** Baboons travel in large, noisy "troops" that might have more than 200 members. That's a lot of baboons!

LOOK BACK

Learning to identify letter sounds (phonemes) at the beginning, middle, and end of words is called "phonemic awareness."

- The word *big* <u>begins</u> with the *b* sound. Listen to the words on page 19 being read again. When you hear a word that <u>begins</u> with the *b* sound, blow bubbles with a bubble wand!
- The word *tub* <u>ends</u> with the *b* sound. Listen to the words on page 31 being read again. When you hear a word that <u>ends</u> with the *b* sound, blow bubbles!
- **Challenge**: Listen to the names in the box below being read. Blow bubbles when you hear the *b* sound in the <u>middle</u> of a word!

Bubba	Bear	Barnaby	Badger
Buster	Buffalo	Bobby	Baboon

TRY THIS!

The Banana Game

- Draw 12 bananas on a sheet of paper. Lightly color the bananas. Cut them out.
- Make a **green** *b* on one banana. Make a **red vowel** (*a, e, i, o, u*) on each of five bananas. Make a **black consonant** (*c, d, j, r, s, t*) on each of the remaining six bananas.
- Make three-letter words with *b* at the <u>beginning</u>, a **vowel** in the <u>middle</u>, and another **consonant** at the <u>end</u>. Sound out the words.
- Now make three-letter words with *b* at the <u>end</u> of the word.
- **JUST FOR FUN**: Help Bobby by counting your bananas, one by one!

(Some words you can make: bat, bed, bet, bit, bud, but; cob, job, rib, rub, sob, sub, tab, tub)

FOR MORE ACTIVITIES, go to Bobby Baboon's website: www.kanepress.com/AnimalAntics/BobbyBaboon
You'll also find a recipe for Bobby Baboon's Blueberry-Banana Smoothies!

32